Adventures of
Countess Pigula

"Her Royal Imagination"

Written
& Illustrated
By Karen Freysinger

Aha! Elora Danan Productions

Library of Congress Control Number:
2006907228

ISBN-13: 978-0-9786729-0-4
ISBN-10: 0-9786729-0-9

Published and distributed by

Aha!

Elora Danan Productions
P.O. Box 428, Estero, FL   33928
(239) 466-2747 TJFKJF@MSN.COM

To order copies, for permissions and
correspondence with the author/illustrator,
you may write to the above address.

First Edition

Printed in China

I would like to dedicate this book to both my husband Tom and my daughter Elora, who's unconditional love and humorous support kept me motivated.

To my mother for having faith in me.

Countess Pigula (our real life guinea pig) deserves a big hand of applause for being my "Guinea Pig" for writing and illustrating this story. Without her, it would not have happened.

Oh, and I can not forget all those special little people in Elora's second grade class of 2005-6 who encouraged me to keep making them laugh.

To Mrs. Baldi, (head of a media department in the Florida public school system) for her generous help in correcting my grammar.

Thank you all!

And if you turn the music on,
she'll sing a song for you.

On her head
she wears a crown
of hair that's white
and hair that's brown.

Why, Countess, it's you, of course.

When she thinks
you're not looking
or simply not around,
she fast fluffs it up
and swirls it around.

For there certainly is not
a finer looking creature
that close to the ground.

Countess Pigula is short and stout and very, very round.

So if you try to pick her up...

In her cage
is a cardboard box
that we know
she calls home.

She has it chewed up
very nice so now,
there is a lot of room.

Once a week
she has a bath.
Warm water
she does prefer.

When
she is done
and squeaky clean,
it is then time to
dry her fur.

This guinea pig will let you know that "The Royal Treatment" she does deserve.

So when you're brushing
out her fur, it is energy
you must not conserve.

Countess Pigula has lots of friends. They all live at our house.

There are dogs.
There are cats.
Thank goodness,
there are
no rats.

Lots of fish,
a turtle and
I think, a mouse.

Once in a while when the weather is nice, you may find the Countess outside.

She likes to sunbathe by the pool as she reads the most recent...

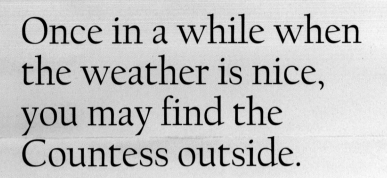

Hey, Countess! Put down that silly magazine and come on in the pool. The water is perfect.

"Guinea Pig Travel Guide"

To keep the Countess
from getting bored,
we gave her a lot of toys.

They klink and
they klank as she rolls
them about.

When it is time to clean her lovely cage of blue, she will want the best above the rest.

No ordinary bedding will do.

Countess Pigula will do the jigula to have you pick her up.

She likes to cuddle in your arms, just like she is a little pup.

Yup!

Oh, just how cool is this!? Yup! Life sure is good. I definitely feel so special in my girl's arms.

This guinea pig
who lives at our house
is very special to us.

She is sweet.
She is kind.
She has stolen
our hearts.

GUINEA PIGS

According to Countess Pigula, guinea pigs are also known as "Cavy". Her ancestors originally came from South America. They are short, sturdy little rodents that are very gentle. They love company, are easy to train and they can be quite active during the day. This makes them a good pet choice for anyone.

Countess Pigula, (like other guinea pigs) likes to talk a lot. She will call to us for many different reasons. Especially when she is hungry. She uses many different sounds to tell us what it is that she wants. She may use squeels, grunts, purrs, whistles, durrs and other sounds. Her favorite is the very loud "WHEEK!"

Not all of these cuties look like Countess Pigula. She says that some have short smooth hair. Some have long curly hair and some have hair that is full of swirls. The last ones she says, just simply look as if they have been in a major wind storm and forgot to brush their hair after they came inside. A guinea pig may be all one color or come in a variety of colors like her.

Guinea pigs love to eat. An activity Countess Pigula would do all day if she could. They need to eat a mix of grains, hay, fresh vegetables, fruits and drink a lot of water. They also need plenty of exercise. A healthy, happy guinea pig may grow up to be eight to ten inches long and live to be five or even eight years of age.

Though her legs are short, she can run very fast. Her front feet have four toes on them and her back feet have three toes on them. Careful trimming of her toe nails regularly, keeps her walking properly. Her ears have very little hair on them and her hearing is very good. Her eyes are set on the sides of her head. This gives her the ability to view a larger area than you or me. Our eyes are in the front of our head. In her mouth are teeth that grow all the time. Chewing on wood or something very hard is necessary to keep her teeth worn down. She does not have a tail, but she does have a tiny little stump where a tail would be.

Countess Pigula likes her cage well ventilated and very clean. As would any guinea pig. She requires the bedding to be absorbent and a few inches deep. Cage size should be approximately two feet by three feet.

When Countess Pigula gets dirty, she likes us to give her a bath in warm, shallow water that is approximately one to two inches deep. We use a shampoo that is made especially for guinea pigs. Afterwards she always reminds us to dry her thoroughly and keep her out of drafts. She doesn't want a cold.

Countess Pigula says that they are wonderful animals. They can become good friends and close family members just as she has become in our home.